W9-BGT-661

CAPTURED!

Arlene Hess Elkins

OMS International
Box A
Greenwood, IN 46142

CAPTURED

Copyright © 2004
Published by OMS International,
Box A, Greenwood, Indiana 46142

All rights reserved. No portion of this book may be reproduced in any form without the written permission of the publisher.

(The text of the original book, *Captured*, copyright 1987, 1992, 1997 by Beacon Hill Press of Kansas City, MO, is included along with additional material which did not appear in the original book. The author granted publication rights to OMS International for this edition, 2004.)

ISBN 1-880-338-38-6

Printed in the United States of America
By Evangel Press, Nappanee, IN

Cover Design: Karen Kresge-Dougherty, Professor, Communication Design; Kutztown University, Pennsylvania

First published by Beacon Hill Press of Kansas City, MO. Inside Illustrations by Doug Bennett. Illustrations used by permission of the original publisher. All rights reserved.

Contents

1. War Comes to the Philippines   7

2. A Home in the Hills   15

3. Life in the Hills   20

4. Leaving Our Jungle Home   30

5. In Zamboanga City   37

6. The Happy Life Blues   41

7. On to Manila   50

8. Los Banos, Here We Come!   60

9. Free at Last!   68

10. Epilogue   80

    Prisoners of War, by R. Bruce Hess   82

    The Miracle of a Song, by Hudson Hess   89

Malayal
Labuan
Tetuan
Zamboanga City

Davao
City

1

War Comes to the Philippines

Pearl Harbor has been bombed!
The United States declares war!

The news came over the radio the morning of December 7, 1941. What did it mean? I didn't know what "Pearl Harbor" was. I knew the United States was my home country. But that was a long way from the village of Tetuan (TET-whan) in the Philippine Islands, where my father and mother were missionaries. I knew the news was bad.

"Mother, will this keep us from having Christmas?" I asked. "You know we haven't bought all our gifts yet."

"I know," Mother answered. "You will want to get something for your brothers and sister. And don't forget Lois's birthday. She will be four years old in just a few days. Try not to worry about Christmas. We will go ahead with our plans and trust the Lord."

"Arlene, let's go outside and play boat," seven-year-old Hudson called to me. He was two years younger than I, and we had fun playing together. Five-year-old Bruce was drawing pictures on the chalkboard.

L to R, parents Viola and Robert Hess. L to R, children Lois, Hudson, Arlene and Bruce.

Mother came to where Hudson and I were playing. "Daddy and I are going to the Bible school to teach," she said. "We'll be home later. Be sure to obey Prosing and Mrs. Chu." Then she hurried after Daddy.

"The news upset Mother," I thought. "I sure hope the bombing of Pearl Harbor doesn't keep us from having Christmas. I can hardly wait!"

Outside it didn't look like Christmas. There was no snow, and it wasn't even cold. But we Hess children always decorated a tree and hung our stockings in a row.

The Filipinos celebrated Christmas their way. We loved it. Children came to our door and sang Christmas carols. They expected to receive coins in return, so we always went to the door to give them some.

Then there were the Christmas lanterns! Made in pastel colors of pink, blue, green, yellow, and lavender, they were so beautiful! Small bamboo sticks were fastened together in the shapes of hollow stars. Colored tissue paper covered the frame.

At night, a lighted candle was placed inside each lantern. They were hung outside around the houses and under the trees. How beautiful they were!

Of course we had our Christmas program at church. I played "Silent Night" on the piano.

I knew the Bible told the story of the first Christmas. God sent His Son to the world. Jesus was the best Christmas present ever given. But that Christmas I was thinking more about the presents I would receive. I hoped the news about Pearl Harbor wouldn't spoil everything.

Right away, though, there were changes. Mother and Daddy got some black construction paper and cardboard. They began cutting and gluing.

"What are you doing?" we asked.

"Every night we have to have blackout," Daddy said. "We have to cover our windows so no light shows from the outside."

"Why can't any light show?" we asked.

Daddy explained, "The Filipinos are afraid the planes that bombed Pearl Harbor might drop bombs here too. If the cities are dark, the pilots of the planes can't find them. That's why we have to cover our windows." It wasn't easy to block out every crack of light.

Soon we saw people digging holes in their yards.

We asked Daddy about that too. He said they were digging air-raid shelters. If enemy planes did come, people could hide in the holes.

"Are we going to dig air-raid shelters too?" we asked.

"Yes," Daddy told us. Several Bible school students came to help dig some near our homes.

But when it rained, the holes filled with water.

"There are a lot of frogs in the holes," Hudson reported one day. We all went to look.

The days passed slowly. Christmas was almost here, but it was hard to buy gifts. Many of the stores had closed. Some storekeepers had sold everything. They were afraid soldiers would come and take their stores. Still we found a few things to buy.

At last Christmas Day arrived! We were delighted to find a child-size set of furniture. There was a couch, two chairs, and a round table. It was just like grown-up wicker furniture, but smaller.

"Where did you hide this furniture, Mother?" I asked. She smiled at me but didn't answer. She kept her hiding place a secret. I thought I knew where the good hiding places were. I had often found gifts in the past. "Where could it be?" I wondered.

On New Year's Day, Mother said she and Daddy were going to have prayer meetings in Mercedes. Prosing, a Bible school student who looked after us, and Mrs. Chu, our Chinese nanny, would stay with us.

"Be good children. We will be back this afternoon," they said.

It was a warm day. Hudson and I went out to play in our backyard while Bruce and Lois took a nap.

"Let's play zoo," I said. "We can put crates over the animals and pretend they are in cages."

"OK," Hudson said. "That sounds like fun." We put the dog and cat and ducks and any chickens we could catch under crates.

"Look at that fierce lion," I said, pointing to the cat.

"And there is a big grizzly bear," Hudson said. He pointed to the dog.

"Do you think we should take them out of their cages for a walk?" I asked. That sounded like a good idea. One by one we took the animals out of the cages and walked them around.

Suddenly we heard the sound of airplanes overhead. They were the ones we were afraid of.

"Come quickly!" Prosing called. "We had better get in the big air-raid hole!"

But the hole had water and mud in it. The frogs were the only ones to jump in. We looked up, and the airplanes were gone.

Mrs. Chu was worried. She left to find her son.

Prosing went into the house. "I will take you children to the home of one of the other missionaries," she said. She got a bag and put some of our things into it. Then we went to the Gulbransons' house. I wished my parents would come.

After a while Mother and Father came back. They looked for us at home. Finally they found us with the other missionaries.

"We were worried about you," Mother said. "Zamboanga City was bombed. We drove bck as fast as we could."

"But we couldn't drive very fast," Daddy continued. "So many people were leaving the city."

"We asked God to take care of you," Mother finished. "We are so glad you are safe."

The next day, the missionaries talked about what we ought to do. The soldiers were coming to where we lived. Should we stay in the city?

After talking and praying about it, the missionaries decided everyone should leave. "Maybe if we go far away, the soldiers won't find us. Then we will be safe for a while," they said.

It was very exciting. All the missionaries were going to leave at night. Some of the girl students from the Bible school were coming with us also. We didn't have to go to bed until very late!

"Arlene and Hudson, please take this pail," Daddy said. "Get some water from the pump in front of the Bible school."

"You mean go there in the dark?" we asked.

"Yes," Daddy said. "The water that comes through our faucets may not be good to drink. When the planes attacked the city, they may have polluted the water. The pump water is from a well. It will be safe."

Hudson and I went quietly through the dark to the pump. We pumped and pumped until the pail was full. Then we carefully carried it back to our house.

A few days later, all the missionaries were packed and ready to leave. After dark we left as quietly as we could.

We rode and rode for many miles. At last we came to a lumber camp. It was at a place called Labuan (LAHB-wahn). We spent the night in a large storehouse called a bodega (bo-DAY-guh). We slept on the floor. It was like camping out. The only lights we had were flickering lamps.

"Lie down and go to sleep," our mothers told us. "Stop talking." But it was so hard to sleep. We were too excited.

The next morning we jumped up from our beds on the floor and ran outside. "Look, there is a little creek," we called to each other. "Mother, can we go and wade?" we asked.

She nodded her head, and we ran toward the creek. The air was cool and sweet. The birds were singing. It was just like the song "This Is My Father's World." It was God's world, and we knew He was near.

2

A Home in the Hills

Soon we couldn't stay in the lumber camp anymore. Some nearby Christian Filipinos invited us to stay in their homes.

After a few days, a boat came to Labuan. "Are we going on a boat ride?" we asked.

"Yes, children," the adults said. "The Lord helped us find the boat. It will take us up the coast to Malayal (muh-LIE-ul)."

Everyone boarded, and we were on our way.

What a hot afternoon it was! Our faces and arms became badly sunburned. Even our lips cracked from too much sun. "This is still a lot more fun than school," we thought.

Many Christians from the church in Malayal came to meet us when we arrived and helped us unload. We were glad for their help.

"Are we going to stay with the Filipinos for a long time, Daddy?" we asked. "We are a long way from home."

"Don't worry," Daddy told us. "God will take care of us. He will help us find a place to stay. Remember, the Bible says, 'God cares for you'" (see 1 Peter 5:7).

"You can put your things in the schoolhouse," the village people told us. "There is no school now. You can live there until you decide what to do."

The Christians at Malayal were very good to us. When it was mealtime, they piled a long table high with good things to eat.

"Let's praise God for His wonderful care for us," one of the missionaries said. "Let's sing 'Come and Dine.'"

I had never heard that song before, but I liked it. The song seemed to say that Jesus knew all about us. He knew we were far from our homes. He would take care of us. He would help us have food to eat and a place to stay, just as He helped people in the Bible long ago.

We stayed in the schoolhouse in Malayal for three weeks.

Some of the missionaries and Filipino Christian men hiked back into the hills to find a new home for us. A trail went beside the Salupit (sah-LOO-pit) River. About two hours down the trail, they found a place for a campsite.

The Filipinos cleared away the jungle bushes and vines. They built houses for us.

One night in the schoolhouse, Mother told me a wonderful secret.

"We are going to have a new baby," she said. "It will be born sometime next August."

I was so excited! But this was only January. August was a long time away. "I hope it is a little sister," I told Mother.

The next day some of the men went to get some more things from our old houses in Tetuan. I remembered our new Christmas furniture and my kitten. I wished Daddy would bring them to our new home.

"Look what we brought with us," they said when they got back.

"Is it our furniture?" I wondered.

"Oh, no," we groaned. "Schoolbooks! Why did you have to bring our schoolbooks? We are having so much fun. We don't want to go to school."

"Don't worry. You won't have to go to school until we get settled in our new home," they told us. Still we knew that our vacation soon would be over.

At last moving day came. We had to walk along the trail into the jungle. Many of the Christian Filipino men carried loads on their heads. They carried our luggage and food and even some furniture. We were glad to have their help once again.

At last we came to our new home. There was a large house ready for us. We had a dining area big enough for all of us to eat together. There were two long tables with benches made out of logs and a roof to keep out the sun and rain.

There was also a shack where the Filipino cook prepared our meals. He built a fire between stones and set the pots of food on the stones to cook.

At first everyone lived in the one big house. It was crowded, but we children didn't mind, and we set off exploring right away. Around three sides of our little camp was a low hill, which we called "the ridge." The men had cut steps into the side of the hill, and we ran quickly up to the top.

"It's neat up here," we called out. "We can see way past the valley." We ran along the ridge, shouting and laughing.

Then we ran down the steps. Down we went, past the big house and the dining shelter—down the path and around a big rock to a creek we called "the river."

"Look at the shrimp in the water," we called out to each other. "And see that deep place where we can swim! We can go swimming every day if we want to!"

"That's right," our mothers told us later. "You can go swimming every day because the river is also your bathtub!"

It wasn't long before we had settled down in our new campsite. Soon we felt right at home.

Before long the big house was overcrowded. "Let's build more houses," some of the missionaries

said. In a little while, we had a small village. The men even built a schoolhouse. But that couldn't keep us from having a lot of fun. Sometimes we missed our home and our Filipino Christian friends. I wondered if my kitten was all right. We were thankful God had taken such good care of us. But we didn't know the danger that was not too far away.

3

Life in the Hills

"Race you to the big rock!" Johnny Gulbranson called. He ran down the path to the river. Behind him came my brother Hudson and Dick Landis.

"I'll be the first one in!" Dick shouted. He held his nose and jumped into the deep pool, feet first. He came up under the rock overhang. Johnny and Hudson jumped in after him.

"We're going to splash in the shallow water," the younger children said. My sister, Lois, Paul Landis, and Larry Snead lay on their tummies and kicked their feet in the water.

"Betty," I called to Betty Gulbranson, "let's go up the river a little where no one is splashing. We might be able to catch some shrimp. We can make little ponds for them."

We collected rocks and made shallow pools of water. We gently guided the shrimp into the "ponds" we had made. Then we put rocks across the entrance.

"Are you catching shrimp?" the boys asked, coming over to watch.

"Go away unless you are going to help," we said. "We want to catch some and roast them over the coals."

"We'll help you," said the boys. Soon we had quite a few shrimp. Our parents helped us build a fire and roast them. Yummy!

When we got tired of the water, we walked upstream along the river. Everything was so beautiful. Wild orchids grew all around us. We swung on the long vines that hung down.

There was a waterfall farther up the river, and sometimes we ate picnic lunches there.

"Tomorrow, some of us boys are going up to the garden," Hudson said one evening. "We will help cut down vines and bushes."

"You better be careful," I said. "Remember when Bruce cut his finger with a bolo (large knife)?"

"Of course we'll be careful," my brother answered. "I'm older than Bruce, anyway."

The Filipinos had helped our fathers build the hillside garden. They had burned down trees and planted corn between the stumps.

21

In the middle of the garden stood a little hut. Wires went from the hut to all parts of the garden. Pieces of cloth hung on the wires. The cloth flapped wildly when the wires were pulled. Someone stayed in the hut and pulled the wires when birds or monkeys came into the garden to eat the corn.

Several times whole troops of monkeys came chattering through the trees along the ridge. We all ran out to watch them go by. There were other creatures in our jungle camp as well. There were snakes! We would see them cross our path as we walked along or see them curled around a tree. One day a big green snake curled itself around the top of a window in one of the houses. It hung down by its tail and swung back and forth!

"Help! There's a snake in the window," someone called. Mr. Landis came running. He was our "official" snake killer. He killed about 20 while we were in the hills.

There were also spiders and centipedes and scorpions. No one was bitten by a snake, but some of us did get spider bites. One morning when I put on my sneaker, I felt a terrible pain in my foot.

"Ouch," I yelled. "Something bit me!" I shook my shoe upside down, and a scorpion fell out. My foot was sore where his pinchers had grabbed me. If he could have swung his tail around and stung me, I would have had a swollen foot for a long time.

One thing we liked to do was collect butterfly wings. I had never before seen so many beautiful butterflies. When they died, we found their shimmering wings everywhere. I filled a can with butterfly wings. It was one of my treasures.

When we were in the hills, we didn't have any

dogs or cats for pets. But we did have another kind of pet.

Sometimes the Filipinos brought chickens for us to eat. Since we didn't have refrigerators, the chickens were tied up until the cook was ready to prepare them for dinner.

Then someone had an idea. "Why not raise chickens ourselves?"

That seemed like a good idea. Several of the fathers built chicken houses to keep the chickens safe at night. My father built a chicken house for our chickens partway up the side of the ridge. Mr. Landis built a house for his chickens too. Soon there were hens strutting around. They clucked at their chicks to follow them as they hunted in the leaves for bugs and worms.

Then we kids got an idea. "Could we each have a chicken for a pet?" we asked. Each of us who wanted a pet was allowed to choose one. I chose a small brown hen and named her Goldenrod.

"Come, Goldenrod," I coaxed, holding out a piece of food. I waited very quietly. After many tries, Goldenrod timidly came and took food out of my hand.

Mr. Holish had chickens for pets too. We loved to see them fly up to his shoulders. "My little doves," he called them. "My palomas." They did look like doves. They were slim and shiny. One was black, and the other two were white. The black one sparkled blue-black in the sun. I thought Mr. Holish had a sort of magic to be able to get his pets to come when he called them.

One day an idea came to me. "Mother, when Goldenrod lays eggs, may I eat them myself?"

Mother thought for a moment. "Well, we need all

23

the eggs we can get. We don't have many places to get food. But you may have the first egg she lays. How's that?"

I was excited. How could I celebrate when I had Goldenrod's first egg? Just eating it for breakfast wasn't special enough. I thought and thought.

Then came the exciting day. I held the small, brown egg in my hand. It was my very own egg, laid by Goldenrod for me. What could I do? Then I knew. I ran to my friend, Betty Gulbranson.

"Betty," I called. "Let's have a party and eat Goldenrod's egg." And that is what we did. Having a party and sharing with a friend made it special.

One night there was a terrible squawking among the chickens. The noise came from the camp chicken house. The men grabbed their flashlights and ran to see what was the matter.

A civet cat was trying to carry off the old Rhode Island Red rooster. He was the "granddaddy" of the chickens.

The men scared the wildcat off. But old Red had only half a comb on the top of his head. He strutted around proudly anyway. He seemed to realize he had won a very unfair fight.

We had a lot of fun at our camp in the hills. It was easy to forget that we were there because of war. But soon something happened that reminded us.

One day in February, my father and several people from our camp went back to Tetuan. They arrived safely and went to sleep in the Bible school building. But in the middle of the night, a man came running and woke them up.

"Enemy ships are coming into the harbor," he shouted. "You had better leave right away."

My father and the other missionaries got up in a hurry. They drove away from the city until the road stopped. They parked the cars and hiked into the hills. That was the last time they saw the cars.

That night they stood on a little hill above the city and watched the ships come into the harbor. They were coming to take over the city. When the missionaries got back to our camp, we knew there would be no more trips to Tetuan for supplies.

The Bible was very important to us in those days. When everyone met for Bible reading and prayer, someone often read from the Psalms.

"Here is a good chapter for us to memorize," someone said. "This would be especially good for the children to learn."

He that dwelleth in the secret place of the most High shall abide under the shadow of the Almighty.

I will say of the LORD, He is my refuge and my fortress: my God; in him will I trust.

Surely he shall deliver thee . . .

He shall cover thee with his feathers, and under his wings shalt thou trust *(Psalm 91:1-4)*.

For many days after that, we worked on memorizing that psalm. It reminded us that God was taking care of us.

"Mother, I wish I could stay up later some night," I said one day. "You know I like to sew. It is hard to go to bed when Lois does every night."

"I will talk with some of the other mothers," Mother said. "We'll see about it."

The mothers decided that the older girls—Patsy Landis, Betty and Peggy Gulbranson, and I—could stay up later on Friday nights.

"Oh, goody," we said. "Shall we wear our night-clothes?"

"You may put on your pajamas and wear your housecoats over them," Mother said. "Then you can go to bed as soon as it is time."

Every evening, after all the children were in bed, the adults gathered in the dining area. There they would read, sew, write, or talk. One bright lamp was lit so everyone could see. We were glad we could join the fun on Friday nights.

Before everyone said good night, we all sang and prayed. A song I liked especially was "Safe Am I."

Safe am I, safe am I, In the hollow of His hand;
Sheltered o'er, sheltered o'er, With His love forever-
more.
No ill can harm me, No foe alarm me, For He keeps
both day and night.
Safe am I, safe am I, In the hollow of His hand.*

That song made me feel so safe. Sitting in the cozy lamplight, we knew that God was with us. His Word, the Bible, said that He was taking care of us. As I looked around, I knew it was true.

Early one morning, I looked out the window of our house toward the ridge. I saw a light moving along the path from the Landises' house to the Loptsons'. Someone was walking along the path with a lantern.

I knew my mother was at the Loptsons', and that it was almost time for our baby to be born. Just then Daddy came into our room.

"How do you like your new brother?" he asked.

How excited we were! Daddy said they had named the baby Victor Glenn—Victor for Victory and Glenn for the mountain glen where we were living.

Little Victor Glenn was born on August 12. Already we had been in our camp more than six months.

When we first arrived, we didn't know how long we would stay. Sometimes we heard that our army was coming to rescue us. We waited and waited. But they didn't come.

The enemy came into Zamboanga City in February. In April our soldiers had surrendered to them. We were alone in our little camp in the hills. Our army could not help us now.

Often it was hard to get food. Our fathers hiked many miles to get sugar and other supplies. Some-

Victor Glenn Hess

27

times a friendly Chinese storekeeper had food we could buy. Other times he had very little.

One day soldiers in the city found out about us. They knew there was a group of missionaries hiding in the jungle.

We heard that they were coming up the coast to get us. While we children slept, our parents dug holes around the camp. They hid our cans of food and other valuables. They had a hard time sleeping for several nights.

Then a surprising thing happened. A terrible storm came up. It was almost like a typhoon. It rained and rained for almost a week. The river rose higher and higher. There was no way anybody could come up the riverbank to get us. Once again God protected us as He said He would in the Bible.

Slowly the days passed. Our parents wondered if the enemy soldiers would come to get us any day soon. Sometimes planes flew over our camp. But they could not see us because of the big trees. When the men built our camp, they didn't cut them down. Now they were glad they hadn't.

It was getting nearer and nearer to Christmas. We had been in the hills nearly a year. How could we have Christmas in the jungle? There were no stores.

We decided to make presents for each other. Soon secrets were whispered all around. The names of everyone in the camp were put in a container. Each person chose one name. He was to make a gift for the person whose name he drew. We began to get more and more excited. But we also knew the soldiers could come to get us before Christmas.

We made gifts out of paper and cloth. Some whittled presents out of small pieces of wood.

The ladies planned the best Christmas dinner they could. It was hard to stay away from the dining area. Everything looked so good! It tasted good too.

When Christmas Day arrived, we gave and opened our gifts. We had a wonderful Christmas dinner. It was almost perfect. We thanked God for His protection. We discovered that Christmas isn't where you are. It isn't even beautiful decorations and store-bought gifts. It's feeling God's love and the love of family and friends. It's knowing God is with you. We knew God was with us this special Christmas in the forest.

*Words to "Safe Am I" by Mildred Leightner Dillon © 1938. Renewed 1966 by William S. Dillon. Used by permission.

4

Leaving Our Jungle Home

After Christmas, a Filipino man named Anjalan (AHN-juh-lahn) told the men, "You may have some cassava roots from my field. All you have to do is come and dig them."

Cassava roots are brown on the outside and white on the inside. After they are peeled, sliced, and dried, they are ground into flour. This makes good cakes and pies.

"I will go and dig the cassava roots," Daddy said. He went and worked for several days. One day as he worked in the cassava field, two Filipino men came up to him. They were the sons of Mr. Johnson, a lumberman from Zamboanga City. The missionaries knew him before the war.

"Hello," the men said. My father was surprised. He wondered why these men had come up into the hills.

"Where is your camp?" they asked. My father pointed in the direction of the camp.

"The enemy soldiers have talked to us," they said. "They told us to take a message to the headman of your mission."

Daddy showed them how to get to our camp, where they talked with Mr. Gulbranson. "The soldiers know where you are," they told him. "They want all of you to come down to Zamboanga City."

The missionaries were troubled. "How can we go down?" they asked each other. "We don't have any boats. What shall we do?

"Let's send a message to the soldiers' leader," they said. "Let's tell him politely that we need more time. We have no way of coming right now."

The Johnson brothers took the message back to the army in Zamboanga City.

The missionaries prayed and talked some more. "Maybe we should send someone into the city," someone said. "They can talk with the soldiers. Maybe they can find some boats and cars to take us into the city."

Three men were chosen. They stood under the trees near the river. "We will put our hands on these men and pray for them," some of the others said. "We will ask God to protect them and bring them back safely."

When the prayer was over, everyone opened his or her eyes. There stood six or seven Filipino army men with rifles. They said, "We have heard that the enemy army leader has asked your group to go down to Zamboanga City."

"Yes, that is right," we said.

"We are soldiers of the Philippine army," the men said. "We think you should not go down into the city. You should come and be protected by our army. We are fighting on your side."

31

Now the missionaries didn't know what to do. Should they do what the enemy leader said? Or should they listen to the soldiers of the Philippine army?

"Well, perhaps the three men shouldn't go down to the city at this time," the missionaries said to each other. Their families were glad they didn't go.

After the Filipino soldiers left, everyone was a little anxious. What would the enemy leader do when he heard our message from the Johnson brothers? Would they come up and get us? Would they be angry?

Then something happened. It began to rain. The wind blew. Water rushed down the Salupit River. For five days it poured rain. The river overflowed and rushed down the sides of the hills.

When it stopped raining, the trail from our camp to Malayal was washed away. No one could come up to our camp. And no one could go from our camp to the city.

"Now the enemy will have a harder time coming up to our camp," the missionaries said. "God has helped us again, just as He promised in the Bible."

After several days, Daddy told Mr. Landis, "Let's go to Mr. Cawa's store. Maybe he has some food we can buy. We'll carry it back in our knapsacks."

"That's a good idea," Mr. Landis said. "But it will take at least two trips."

At the end of the first trip, Daddy rinsed his knapsack in the river and laid it over a log to dry. "Tomorrow I will make another trip to the store," he said.

He got up early the next morning. The sun was just coming up. He went down to the river to get his knapsack.

As he came back up the little path, he looked up toward the ridge. There was a man coming down the long steps from the top of the ridge. A long line of men followed close behind him.

The leader came up to Daddy. "Halt!" he said.

The enemy soldiers had found us!

"You are all to get ready at once," the leader said. "You will leave in two hours."

Right away other missionaries came out of their houses. They saw the enemy soldiers. They knew there wasn't much time to get ready.

It was almost time for breakfast. "Come, children," the mothers called. "Come and eat some breakfast. We will have something special this morning."

The mothers opened cans of peaches. How wonderful it was to have peaches. We didn't have them very often. But the peaches didn't taste very good this morning. My stomach didn't feel like eating.

Everyone rushed around trying to get ready. Patsy and I watched the soldiers. "They are catching our chickens," we said. The soldiers had built little fires. They were cooking our chickens and putting the meat into their canteens.

"I hope they don't get Goldenrod," I said. "I think Daddy opened the chicken house door early this morning. He let our chickens out before they came."

"Arlene!" Mother called. "Go to each of our beds. Open up the cloth mattresses. Shake out the grass from each mattress. I want to take the mattress coverings with us. When we get to the next place we are to stay, we will fill the mattresses again."

I knew what Mother meant. Our mattresses were really just great big sacks. When they were filled with dried grass, they were soft to sleep on.

I emptied each mattress and hung the sacks over the porch railing. Then I ran down the stairs and outside to see what was going on.

It was almost time to go. Only an hour had passed, but the soldiers were ready. Everyone put on a knapsack. Every mother had made each person in her family a knapsack. This way we could all help carry our clothes and other possessions down to the city. Even the smaller children had knapsacks.

"Let's take as much food with us as we can," we said to each other. Everyone had big loads. But there were two boxes of canned evaporated milk left.

"Who is going to carry these boxes?" one of the soldiers asked. No one had any more room. So he dropped the boxes on the ground. They split open and milk cans rolled out.

"Quick," one of the ladies said. "You children, pick up the cans. Put them in your knapsacks." Soon all the cans had been picked up.

Now it was time to start down the trail. We went single file. The children ran and slipped and circled around. For some of us it was great fun. Sometimes we looked down over steep cliffs.

"Hey, guys," Dick suddenly shouted. "Come and look." We ran to see what it was. "Look over the edge of the cliff." There was a can of evaporated milk. It had fallen out of Dick's knapsack as he had leaned over the edge. Down, down it bounced and tumbled. Then it bounded out of sight.

Dick turned back to the trail, his eyes shining, "That was fun!" he said.

Sometimes the trail was scary. Once we had to cross a log. A stream trickled far below. The soldiers had no trouble crossing it. They were used to these

paths. But we went over it very carefully.

My mother carried little Victor. He looked fat. Mother had wrapped as many diapers around him as she could. This was a way to carry the diapers.

But when she saw the log bridge, she looked

around and saw there was no one near to help her, no one except a soldier with a gun.

Mother turned to him. "I'm afraid to carry my baby across the log," she said. "I might fall. You are used to walking on logs like this. Will you carry my baby across?"

"I will if you will carry my gun," the soldier replied. He took the baby. Mother took his gun. The soldier carried the baby until the path was safe again.

Right then Bruce came running up. He saw Mother without Victor and became very frightened. "Where is our baby?" he asked. "What happened to our baby?"

But then he saw the soldier with Victor.

After a few hours, we all got down to the sea-coast and waited for the boats to come for us.

While we waited, we ate some lunch. Mother opened a can of fruit. We had some homemade crackers.

We looked around and saw the soldiers enjoying chicken dinner on the beach.

"Here come the boats," someone called. Five or six people got into each one. Then we sailed down the coast to Labuan, where just a year before we had stayed overnight in a lumber camp.

We spent the night in some Filipino homes. Early the next morning we got on trucks and rode into Zamboanga City. Where were we going to stay this time?

5

In Zamboanga City

On went the trucks through the city. At last they stopped in front of a building. It was the Philippine police barracks. The Philippine army used to stay there. Now it was our new "home."

The adults soon decided where everyone would sleep. Then we unpacked our belongings.

"We must get out the mosquito nets and bedding for the night," people were saying.

The soldiers were watching us.

"Put all your books and magazines in the middle of the floor," they said. "Give us your pens, pencils, and penknives."

We looked at each other. "That means our Bibles and New Testaments too," we said. Sadly we picked up our precious Bibles. We laid them gently on the floor. It didn't seem possible. Did we really have to give our Bibles away? What would we do without them? We were glad we had hidden some of the words in our hearts by memorizing them.

The soldiers took the Bibles and other things to their headquarters.

Soon we were tucked into bed. Before going to sleep, we prayed, "Please, dear God, help us get our Bibles back. Help us to read and obey them better than ever before. Amen."

The next morning, the children got up early. We wanted to explore our new surroundings. There was a lot of "junk" around that soon became "treasure" to us. We had fun.

Several days passed. We missed our Bibles and New Testaments.

"Let's ask the soldiers if we can have our Bibles back," Mr. Clingen said one day. "We need them so much. Maybe if we make a special request, they will give them back."

So the special request was made. One day the soldiers brought the Bibles back. "You may have the 'Holy Bibles,'" they said. "But you cannot have the

'New Testaments.'" We were happy. We didn't let on that the Bibles had both the Old *and* New Testaments!

The Lord worked out something else special too. The soldiers let the missionaries go to the Filipino markets with a guard. When they got to the market, the guard disappeared for a while. The missionaries could walk around the marketplace. They could talk to many of their friends who were there. They found out what had been happening while we were up in the hills. They found out how God had been helping the Filipino Christians who had been living in the city.

As the days went by, we wondered how long we would be staying here. Sometimes we heard rumors that the soldiers would take us to another city many miles away. It was called Davao (DAH-vow) City.

One day the rumor came true. We were going to Davao City! Time to pack.

We traveled to Davao City on a ship. We slept one night in the deepest part of the ship, called the "hold." It was just a big storage place with a big covering. We were glad we had to stay there only one night.

Zamboanga City

Davao City

6

The Happy Life Blues

"Look at all the people," we said to each other in Davao City. They all lived in one building that had once been a dance hall. It was called the Happy Life Blues.

We carried our luggage up the steps and into the building. "We have made room for you," the people said. "Here is your space." We looked around. All we could see was a big, empty dance floor.

"Now we will show each of you where you will live. This part of the floor is for the Landis family. This part of the floor is for the Gulbranson family. And this part of the floor is for the Hess family."

How strange it all was. How could a certain part of the floor be the place where we lived? But that was the way it was.

"Well, I guess we will have to string some rope for our mosquito nets tonight," our mothers and fathers said. "Tomorrow we will see what we can do to make our floor space more homelike."

The next day, people hung blankets and sheets for dividers. The little children loved to run down the length of the floor. They ran through the dividers one after another.

Some children thought it was fun to lift one corner of the blanket and look inside another family's home. It was hard to have to be so close together. When the babies and children cried, it was very noisy and hard to sleep.

"I wish you hadn't left the mattress sacks hanging over the railing in the hills, Arlene," Mother said. "Now I will have to make some more. Then you children must gather grass and fill them so we can have soft beds."

"I think we will have to make some beds and chairs," the men said to each other. "Our living space is very close to the front door. The children come running in with their muddy feet. They walk all over the bedding and luggage. Maybe the soldiers will let us go and gather some materials."

The soldiers gave permission for small groups of men to leave the camp. Right after breakfast the men and boys lined up in front of the sentry and bowed. Then they went to the swamp and cut down small trees and bamboo.

Soon there was enough material to make furniture. "What are you going to make first, Daddy?" we asked.

"Well, I think I'll make beds," he said. "First, a double bed for mother and me. Then a double-decker for Arlene and Lois and Hudson and Bruce. And finally, a crib for Victor."

"Can Lois and I sleep on the top bunk?" I asked. I remembered that up in the hills Hudson and Bruce slept on top.

"I think you two should sleep on the bottom,"

Daddy answered. "Maybe next time we move, you can sleep on the top.

"I will fasten a pole down the center of each bed. That will help you to stay on your own side."

Next Dad made a table and some chairs. Then Mother had an idea. "Do you think you could make a high chair for Victor?" she asked.

"I don't know," Daddy answered. "I've never made one before."

"I'll figure out how you can do it," Mother said. And she did. Dad followed her idea and made the high chair. It was a great help for Victor.

We had a much bigger camp to explore this time. There were about 264 people in it. A big, grassy area separated the dance hall and the main road. A driveway went from the building to the road past the sentry's little shelter. No one went out without permission.

Inside camp a water pipe stood up out of the ground. At the end of the pipe was a faucet. The people in camp washed their dishes there. Sometimes the water pressure was low. Then we pushed the faucet over until the pipe was lying on the ground.

Sometimes the water went off. If we were in the middle of soaping our clothes or washing dishes, it was just too bad. We had to wait until the water came on again. And sometimes that was two or three hours later!

Our shower was a small building outside in the yard. A pipe with a showerhead came out of the ground. The walls were palm leaves. There was no roof.

One day I was in the shower house when a baseball came crashing through the palm leaf walls.

"Quick, throw the ball over the wall," someone said. "If you don't, someone might come in after it!" I quickly grabbed the ball and threw it outside.

At the new camp, everyone had chores to do. There were different crews of people to do different jobs.

There was a cooking crew. Those people fixed meals in the big camp "kitchen." It was made of palm leaves. Food was put in big pots to cook over fires.

There was a coconut milk crew. These people prepared coconut milk each morning to eat on our cooked cereal. They split coconuts in half and then grated the white part. They added water to the grated coconut and squeezed it into a container. The liquid was white and looked exactly like milk. It tasted delicious on cereal.

There were many other crews, including a sanitary crew. These people collected garbage and trash. They kept our camp as clean as possible.

Even the children had chores to do (all except the little ones). We had to weave coconut fronds. Father Vasina, a Catholic priest, explained our job to us. Father Vasina's chore was to organize the children to do their chores.

"Every evening, right after supper, all of you will come out here in front of the big building," he said. "Each of you will be given a coconut frond. I will show you how to weave the frond leaflets in a special way."

"What are the woven fronds for?" a child asked.

"The men will use them to make walls and roofs of buildings in our camp," Father Vasina answered. "Old fronds turn brown and split and crack. The men need new ones to replace them. It will be your job to make sure new ones are ready to use."

"That doesn't sound like much fun to me," one of the children grumbled. "I don't think I'm going to like weaving fronds."

But Father Vasina wasn't finished explaining.

"After you each weave a certain number of fronds, we will play games together," he said. That sounded like fun. We hurried to get our fronds woven as quickly as possible.

One of the games we liked best was crack-the-whip. If you were at the very end of the long line of children, you had to hold on extra tight.

Another thing the children spent a lot of time doing was standing in line at mealtime. Some parents sent their children to hold a place in line a long time before the food lines opened. That way they got their food without having to wait so long.

If you were holding a place in a food line, you didn't leave. You stood there so no one else would get ahead of you. We used to play games while we waited. One game was stone, paper, scissors. Groups of two would play the game. The child who won would slap the other child's wrist as hard as he could with two fingers. The wrists of children who had played a long time were bright red.

One day Daddy said to us, "We are going to be moving." Of course we wanted to know where.

"We won't be moving out of the camp," Father said. "Some of the people in our big building have moved out. The soldiers have given them permission to build little houses out of coconut fronds nearby. That leaves more room for us. We will move from the big dance floor to the mezzanine floor." The mezzanine floor was something like a large balcony.

How nice it was to have our own section away

from the front door. But even here we had to keep as quiet as possible. Many old men lived nearby. They didn't like to hear babies and children crying. If they heard someone cry, they would shout, "Shut him up! Choke him!" It was hard to keep the children quiet.

Sometimes Mother said to me, "Arlene, go and pat Victor's back so he will go to sleep. If he cries, other people will be upset."

So I would kneel beside the crib and reach my hand through the bars. I would pat and pat Victor's back. Sometimes it seemed he would never go to sleep.

Every day after the noon meal, we had siesta time. Everyone in the whole camp had to be very quiet for about an hour. Some people took naps. Others read quietly. The children found quiet things to do.

My friend Cecily and I liked to spend siesta time sitting on a blanket under a tree. One day when we were sitting there, something fell from the coconut tree above us. It was part of the tree and felt something like burlap.

"Look, Cecily," I said. "I bet I could make a pair of sandals for Victor out of this. If I line it carefully with cloth, it won't rub his feet."

Cecily thought it was a good idea. So did Mother when I told her about it later. I stood Victor on a piece of paper and traced around his feet. Then I cut the coconut fiber from the pattern. I cut pieces for straps and sewed cloth on the back of each piece.

The sandal project took several siestas, but finally I was done. How proud I was when Victor wore the sandals I had made him.

One day Daddy said, "How would you like for us to have our own house instead of living in this large building?"

"That would be fun," we said.

46

"Well," Daddy went on, "Mother and I have been talking with Mr. and Mrs. Bressler. They would like to live in their own house. We thought we could build a house together. Their family would live in one side, and we Hesses would live in the other."

"We could call it the 'BressHessler Duplex,'" someone said.

Then Father talked with us some more. "If the soldiers let us build this house, everyone will have to work. Mr. Bressler and I will have to go and get the poles and coconut palms. You children will have to weave many, many fronds. This will be in addition to the ones you weave for the camp. Are you willing to do this?"

We all said yes. All we could think of was the BressHessler Duplex. What fun it was to see the building go up piece by piece! We worked hard at weaving fronds.

One day our house was finished. We were proud to move in. That was a wonderful day.

Everybody tried to keep busy and happy at camp. It was hard to be prisoners. It was hard not to be able to go where we wanted to go. It was hard eating food we didn't like.

But people tried to be cheerful and to cheer other people up. Many of the people in our camp were Christians. They planned Sunday School and church services each Sunday. Cecily's mother taught the children Bible verses and hymns. I liked the new songs I learned. One was

Sun of my soul! Thou Savior dear,
It is not night if Thou be near.
Oh, may no earthborn cloud arise
To hide Thee from Thy servant's eyes!

—John Keble

Some of the good singers in the camp put on concerts in the evenings. One group was called a barbershop quartet. Mr. Snead from our group was in that quartet. We liked to hear them sing spirituals and other fun songs.

There were many songs and jokes about the Happy Life Blues. People made up songs about the food. One of them was called "Father Abbott's Chowder." Father Abbott was one of the cooks. Someone wrote about his chowder: "Every spoonful makes a tuneful; / Makes you sing the louder."

The soldiers let Filipinos come to our camp to sell food. Daddy bought peanuts from one of the Filipinos.

"You children can help make peanut butter for our family," he told us. "First, we have to shell all these raw peanuts. Each of you will shell a certain amount each day. Arlene and Hudson will shell two cups each. Bruce and Lois will shell one cup each. At the end of each day I will ask you if you shelled your amount of peanuts.

"In the earlier days in America, a job like this was called a 'stint,'" Daddy told us. "Now each of you will do your stint for the day."

It was hard to shell so many peanuts every day. But after Daddy roasted the peanuts and ground them in a food chopper, we all enjoyed the peanut butter. Victor called it "peantoo buttie."

We had arrived at the Happy Life Blues in February. The days and weeks went by, and soon it was August 12. Victor was one year old. He learned to walk there in the camp.

Every morning there was roll call. The whole camp gathered together on the lawn in front of the big building. The soldiers walked up and down in front of us. They made sure everyone was there. Sometimes roll call took an hour or more.

The months went by. We heard that maybe our whole camp would be moved. We might go to the city of Manila, way up north. It would take many days to get there by boat.

Every day at roll call we wondered: "Is today the day? Will the soldiers announce, 'Get ready to go to Manila'?"

But the days went by, and we didn't hear anything about it.

Another Christmas was getting nearer. People thought we might stay here until after Christmas.

Soon wonderful rumors began to go around the camp. We heard the grown-ups were planning a special Christmas for all of us. There was to be a toy for every child in the camp. The cooks were planning the best treats they possibly could make.

"I can hardly wait until Christmas," the children said to each other. "The grown-ups are so busy making secret things. I can hardly bear to wait!"

It got closer and closer to Christmas. We almost forgot about going to Manila. Surely we would spend Christmas this year at the Happy Life Blues.

But it was not to be. A couple of days before Christmas, the announcement came at roll call. "Today you will pack your baggage. Have it ready by noon today. It will be taken to the ship this afternoon. You will sleep here tonight. Tomorrow morning, early, you will be taken to the ship. You are going to Manila!"

7

On to Manila

We could hardly believe it! Go to Manila! Now? Just before Christmas?

What about the treats that were already made? What about the good meat we were going to have for Christmas dinner? What about the gifts for every child in the camp?

We were all sad, but there was nothing we could do about it. Maybe we could take the treats with us on the ship. The soldiers said we could put the beef in the ship's refrigerator. Maybe we could still have a celebration.

But now there was little time to think about Christmas. We had to get packed by noon. We would spend only one more night in Davao—only one more night in the BressHessler Duplex. We really hadn't lived in it very long.

When I woke up early the next morning, I heard quiet talking. Mother and Daddy were packing their overnight things in a small bag.

"You children stay in bed," they told us. "We will tell you when it is time to get up."

I sleepily watched from the top bunk. My sister was still asleep beside me. The sun hadn't come up yet. Only a lamp glowed. I felt cozy and safe. I knew my mother and father were taking care of us. Their trust in God helped me feel that God cared for me too.

Outside we waited for the trucks to come. It was cool and dark.

Soon we were riding through the morning light to the ship in Davao harbor. "Where will we stay on the ship, Daddy?" we asked.

"I don't know," he said. "Remember the ship we came on from Zamboanga City to Davao? We were down in the hold that time. I hope it will be better on this ship. We will be traveling four or five days."

Daddy was right about the hold. We went down ladders into the bottom of the ship. There were no cabins. All around the walls were deep shelves. You couldn't stand up in them. You could only sit or crawl back on them to sleep.

We found out where our space was; it was on the floor under one of the shelves. Above us was another shelf where other people were staying.

When night came, I asked Daddy, "Where is my pillow?"

"You can put your head on this life preserver," Daddy said. I laid my head down and was soon fast asleep.

At night it was pitch-dark in the hold when they put the cover on. It was like being down in a hole with a cover on top. It was hot and scary. Sometimes rats ran across us.

During the day, the cover was lifted off. We could go up on deck whenever we wanted to. We soon got used to running up and down the ladders.

On Christmas Eve we were all lying down in the dark hold for the night. Suddenly we heard singing. Some of the missionaries were singing Christmas carols.

Some people didn't like it. They said angry words. I guess they thought we shouldn't celebrate Christmas in the hold of a prisoner ship.

But the singing went on. Soon the quartet began to sing. They sang carol after carol.

I lay there in the darkness listening. The singing was so beautiful! I wished it would never stop. I wanted to go to sleep listening to the music.

You can celebrate Christmas anywhere. You don't need decorations or presents. The Bible tells about the first Christmas. Jesus was born in a stable and laid in a manger. It probably was dark in the stable too. So if Christmas could happen in a stable, it could happen in the hold of a ship.

Suddenly there was a different sound. Somehow a soldier had gotten into our section of the ship. He was drunk, but he was trying to sing.

Then some of the people began to sing, "Show him the way to go home. . . ."

"Oh, no!" I thought. "That will spoil the music." And that is what happened. In a few minutes, some of the officers came and took him out of our section. No one sang any more Christmas carols after that.

But the memory was still there. God was close that Christmas.

On Christmas Day, the adults set the treats out around the deck. But now everyone was so sad about spending Christmas in the hold of a ship that no one felt much like eating the treats.

Of course, many of us knew that Christmas wasn't really the place you were or the kind of celebration you had. We knew that God was with us even in the hold of a ship. But it surely was a different kind of Christmas than we'd ever had before.

"Look at the fire hoses!" someone suddenly shouted. Everyone looked. The hoses were turned on. Water was gushing onto the decks.

"Why did they turn on the hoses? Is there a fire?" we asked.

There wasn't any fire. The hoses were our new showers! In a few minutes all the children were jumping in the water. We screamed and splashed and laughed. It was fun!

But the water was from the ocean. It was salty. When you got dry, you felt sticky. There wasn't any fresh water on the ship to wash with. There wasn't even any to drink. The soldiers loved to drink hot tea. They had a large container of fresh, hot tea. It was the only fresh, hot water there was.

My mother longed for fresh water to wash with. She didn't like the sticky salt water from the fire hoses. Where could she get fresh water?

Then she saw the hot tea container. The tea was fresh and hot. It was not very strong.

Mother got an idea. Just before going down into the hold for the night, she filled a container with hot tea. After the cover was put on over us, she took a sponge bath with the hot tea. It made her feel good so she could sleep better.

After about five days, the ship docked in Manila harbor. We had arrived safe and sound.

Some trucks came to take us to our new camp. This time it wasn't a jungle camp or even a dance hall. It was a university, called Santo Tomás. Here there were many more people than at Happy Life Blues. Many stayed in the university buildings. Many more had built little huts, called shanties, all around the big buildings. They called it Shantytown.

We had to give our names and check in. Then we were shown where we would live. What an unhappy surprise—the men and boys would sleep in a different building from the women and girls and babies.

Daddy, Hudson, and Bruce were shown their room and beds in the main building. Mother, Lois, Victor, and I were in a large room in the dining hall. Many other women and girls and babies were in our room.

During the day our family could be together. Only at night we had to be apart. Mother and Daddy

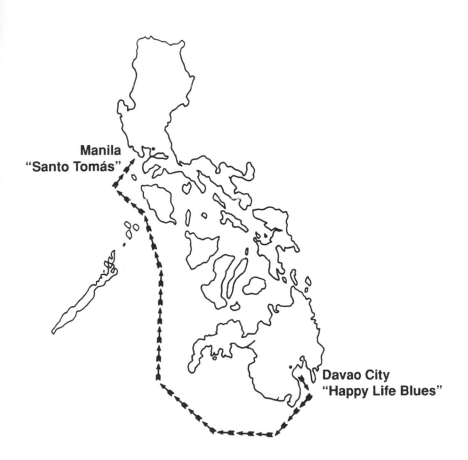

Manila
"Santo Tomás"

Davao City
"Happy Life Blues"

never were happy with this arrangement. What if something happened during the night? We might not find each other in the dark.

We arrived at Santo Tomás just a few days after Christmas. There were still Christmas celebrations going on. I heard there was to be a Christmas party for all the children. How excited I was until I learned it was for children 10 years old and younger. That left me out. My sister and brothers all went, while I watched the fun from a distance.

But something so exciting happened that I almost

forgot my disappointment over the Christmas party. Each person in our Davao group received a big box of food. The boxes had been prepared by the American Red Cross. The prison camp officials let us have them. Each one weighed 48 pounds!

What joy to look inside each box and see the good things to eat. They were all in cans—butter, jelly, corned beef, Spam, powdered milk, powdered coffee, and many other things. Our family received seven boxes, one for each of us. Daddy and Mother carefully chose what food we would eat. We didn't know how long it would be before we could leave the camp. Our parents wanted the food to last as long as it could.

We were thankful to the Red Cross and to the Lord for these wonderful boxes of food.

We soon found that the food in the food line wasn't as good as we had been used to before. There were several food lines: a line for children and young people; a babies' food line; and an adult food line. But in all the lines, the food was tasteless. Sometimes we had fish cakes made of ground fish, bones and all!

With so many people crowded together and poor food, people got sick more often. Once I got dengue fever. I tossed and turned all night because I was so hot and itched so badly. A dim light was burning in the dining hall, so it wasn't dark. But I thought daytime never would come.

Later, all the children in our family except Bruce got the measles. We had to go and stay in the infirmary. Lois and I were in a big room with many other sick children. Our mothers were allowed to come and see us for only a short while each day. I missed my mother.

Hudson had some kind of blood disease; no one ever figured out what it really was. He had to have his blood tested every day. He was in a different room, and we didn't see him for quite a while.

Victor was in a great big room full of baby cribs. The babies cried and cried. The nurses didn't want the mothers to come very often because the babies would cry so hard when they left.

One day Mother was walking past the babies' room when she heard a baby crying. She listened. Yes, it was Victor. She looked in the window. He was standing in his crib, crying his heart out.

Mother couldn't stand to go on by and leave him. She went right into the room and comforted him. The nurses didn't say anything to her.

One day we heard more exciting news. Packages had come from our families and friends back home. The prison soldiers let the Red Cross bring the packages to us.

We could hardly believe it. A Christmas package for each of us from home?

We waited eagerly with many others to hear our names called over the loudspeaker.

Daddy went closer to listen. He didn't want to miss any Hess names being called.

Suddenly he heard "Victor Hess" over the loudspeaker.

"Victor Hess," he said to himself. "How does anybody in the States know about Victor? He was born after the war started. We weren't able to send any letters to our families in the States."

Then he remembered a man who had come up to our camp in Malayal for a short time. Daddy had given him a message about Victor: If you get away from here and get to Australia, please try to send word to my parents in the States. Until that moment, we didn't know whether the man had sent the message or not.

Now Victor had his own package from the States. And after a while, the rest of us got our packages.

Kind friends had chosen the gifts for me. There was a new dress and other clothing. There were soap and toothpaste. And there were sewing needles and different colors of thread. I was thrilled. Now I had pretty colored thread to sew my doll clothes with.

Each member of the family had clothes and toys picked out just for them. We were grateful to our friends back home, and to the Red Cross and the enemy army for letting these packages come to us.

The days went on. It was getting very hot in Manila. It was very hot inside the main building where Daddy, Hudson, and Bruce slept at night. Mother and Daddy still worried about what might happen if our soldiers came to rescue us in the night. Would we find the rest of our family?

There were some other families who felt the same way. We wondered if something could be done about this.

Then we found out about another camp several miles away from Manila. It was not so crowded, and families could stay together.

We asked the soldiers if we could go to this other camp, called Los Banos. They gave permission, and our family got ready to make another move.

But then we remembered Hudson was still sick in the hospital. Would that keep us from going to Los Banos?

Muntinglupa (New Bilibid Prison)
Los Banos
Manila

8

Los Banos, Here We Come!

"How can we go to Los Banos?" we asked. "We can't leave Hudson behind."

"I don't know how the Lord will work it out," Daddy said. "He knows how much we want to live in a place where we can be together. Let's trust Him."

The Lord did work it out. At the very last minute, some good news came. One of the trucks would have cots for the sick people whose families wanted to move to Los Banos. So we all could go to Los Banos after all.

The trip took one day. When we arrived, we saw the buildings were different from the other camps we had been in. There were many of them, long and narrow, with rooms on each side of a long hallway. Between each building, or barracks as we called them, was a washhouse. Everything looked clean and new. We were happy because we could all be together again.

As we carried our luggage to our new home, we passed by barracks where others lived. In front of one building, some flowers bloomed.

"Look, children," said Mother. "There are some four-o'clocks. Collect some of the seeds. I will plant them beside our new house." Quickly we gathered some of the round, black seeds.

The people in charge showed us which rooms were ours. The rooms were called cubicles, and two people were to live in each one. For our family of seven, we were given three and a half cubicles.

The first few nights we slept on the floor, as we had done so often before. As soon as possible, Daddy and the other men went out to get small trees and bamboo to make furniture, as they had done in Davao. Soon there was a double bed and a crib in one cubicle and two double-decker beds in another cubicle. In between was our one-and-a-half cubicle living room, with chairs and a table.

Then the men of our barracks thought of a way to get even more room for each family. They got materials and built another roof on each side of each building. Under our new roof, we put our dining table and chairs. Later, Daddy built a little cookshack nearby.

Mother always loved plants and flowers. It wasn't long before she planted a hedge along our dining area. From the roof above, she hung four or five orchid plants. She even decorated the cookshack with flowers.

"Hudson and I want to plant a small garden between the cookshack and our dining area," Daddy said. "We want to plant lima beans around the cookshack so they will grow up over it."

"That's all right," Mother said. "But let's have something pretty too. I'll plant morning glories to grow up one side and over the top." So we had beans to eat and lovely blue flowers to look at.

Daddy and Hudson planted the small garden. One thing they planted was sword beans. They were long and flat, and that's how they got their name.

Hudson also had a garden farther away from where we lived. He went there almost every day to take care of it. The food from the garden helped because the food line portions kept getting smaller and smaller.

Everyone in camp had a job, just like in Davao. Some worked in the camp gardens all around our camp. Daddy's job was to distribute extra food from the camp garden to all the babies and children in our barracks and the one on the other side of the washhouse.

Every morning he laid the vegetables—tomatoes, squash, eggplant—out on the hard dirt floor of our dining area. Then he divided them evenly so each child would have a share. After that he went up and down the hallways and knocked on each door to deliver the food. Sometimes we would help him.

Soon after we arrived in Los Banos, we went to school. People who had been teachers before the war were asked to teach us. That was their job in camp.

By this time, all our shoes had worn out. We couldn't go barefoot because we would get hookworm in our feet. So we went to a man who made us wooden clogs. We called them *bakias* (BAHK-yuz).

One day Daddy took me to the bakia man. "Stand on this board," the man said to me. When I had done so, he traced around each foot.

"Come back in a couple of days, and I will have your bakias ready," he told us. When we went back, he had cut soles the shape of my feet from the wood. He had nailed on a piece of rubber inner tube for a strap. It was like wearing a wooden slipper.

I thanked the bakia man, and Daddy paid him. When I had worn the bakia's soles thin, I went back to the bakia man for another pair.

When we first got to Los Banos, we had enough food to eat. There was a food line for everyone in the camp. We also had vegetable gardens. The soldiers allowed us to buy eggs and fruit from Filipinos who came to the camp.

But one day some airplanes flew over the camp. "Are those enemy planes?" people asked. We tried to see if the enemy markings were on the wings. "Those aren't enemy planes," someone answered. "They are from an aircraft carrier." Could they be our planes?

Things began to change at camp. First the soldiers said they were making our camp smaller. In one week, the gardens around our camp would be out-of-bounds.

Quickly people began transplanting the vegetable plants from the gardens to places inside the camp. They put the plants anywhere they could. How sad it was to see the little tomato plants, wilted in the sun, trying to grow along the paths where we walked.

A short time later, the soldiers said there would be no noon meal prepared by the kitchen crew. Everyone would have to get lunch from wherever he or she could. And no more Filipinos could come in and sell food.

Little by little there was less food in the lines. We had to find food wherever we could for our lunches. There was a kind of weed growing around where we lived called pigweed. It had prickly bristles on it, but when the bristles were taken off, we cooked and ate the leaves. So the children were sent out to find and pick pigweed.

When bananas were brought into camp, someone got the idea of frying the peelings! We used coconut oil that had been used to make soap to fry them in. That made our throats burn. But we were so hungry that even banana peelings didn't taste too bad.

One of the things we had for most every meal was cornmeal mush. Sometimes we wished we never had to see mush again. Mother had a hard time eating mush meal after meal. So Father made it into pancakes and baked them for her.

My brother Bruce figured out a way to make more food out of what he had in his dish.

Carefully, he poured a little water on his mush. Then he ate the soupy part with his spoon, pushing the larger kernels of corn aside. Then he added more water and ate the watery mush. After a while, he had only clean, washed kernels of corn left. Then, very slowly, he ate each kernel one by one. That way he stretched his food and made it seem like more. We tried his way too.

It seemed longer and longer between meals. Many times during the day I ran over to the other barracks to look at a clock in the hall. I knew it was much too early for the food line, but I could hardly wait. I was so hungry.

It was hard to see Victor in his high chair, reaching out his hand and crying for more food. Mother and Daddy gave him some of theirs, because they couldn't bear to see him cry.

It was hard to go to bed hungry too. One day Daddy had an idea.

"How would it be," he said, "if we saved some of our supper mush and had it before going to bed?"

That sounded like a good idea. So Daddy took

some of the little butter and jelly cans from our empty Red Cross boxes—one for each of us—and put a little mush in each. He put the cans on the shelf in the cook-shack. When it was time for bed, we had our Bible reading and prayer. Every night we prayed, "Lord, please help us have enough to eat to be full again." Then we took our little can of mush and slowly ate every bite. It tasted good.

Now, instead of food lines, a big pot of soup or mush was brought to the door of every other barracks. We lined up with our tin buckets, and someone ladled the food out of the big pot.

Eagerly I watched as seven ladles of food were put into our tin bucket. Sometimes I would hurry back to our table. "The ladles were full tonight," I would say. "See how much fuller our bucket is than it was last night?" Sometimes the ladles were not quite full; then our bucket didn't have as much food in it.

Daddy would fill the little cans and then put food in each of our bowls. Daddy let us children take turns cleaning out the bucket with our fingers, so not one tiny bit of food was wasted. When it was my turn, I ran my finger all around the inside of the bucket and then licked it off.

Along with less food, something else also changed. Airplanes began flying over the camp more and more often each day. They were our planes. We were excited to see them.

We would run out and look up when the planes went over. "Maybe our soldiers will soon come and rescue us," we said. But it seemed that day would never come.

The enemy soldiers didn't like it when we looked up at the airplanes. They were afraid to be seen and ran under the edge of the roof. They told us not to look when the planes went over.

Each day more and more planes flew over. We saw fewer and fewer enemy planes. One day an enemy plane flew over so low it barely missed the fence around our camp. A short distance away it crashed to the ground. That was the last enemy plane we saw over our camp.

When our planes flew over, sometimes they would tip their wings. That made us happy. We were sure the pilots knew we were there. We hoped they would come and get us soon.

As it got closer and closer to Thanksgiving and Christmas, food became scarce. People got thinner and thinner. Many people got sick, and every day people died.

It was hard to be thankful at Thanksgiving time. But Daddy read some verses from the Bible. Habakkuk 3:17-18 showed us that we could praise the Lord even when there was no cow in the stall and no food in the garden. We kept praying for our soldiers to come. We kept trusting in the Lord.

Christmas came nearer. We heard there were more Red Cross boxes on the way and prayed we would get them soon.

"I heard they are on a train not far away," someone said. We hoped and prayed that the enemy soldiers would give us the boxes. But we never got them.

The day after Christmas, Daddy went to the camp hospital for an operation. Mother was weak and not feeling well. Each of us children helped all we could. I washed clothes for our family. I stood on a stool in front of the water trough and scrubbed the clothes on a scrub board. There were a lot of clothes for seven people. Sometimes kind ladies helped me.

Hudson helped cook meals. And Bruce went to the gardens whenever he could to get okra, squash, beans, and talinum (something like spinach). Some days he found only one okra pod and a handful of beans. But every little bit helped.

Another of my jobs was giving Victor a bath. When the water was running, I took him to the bathroom and put him in the big metal trough right beside the faucet. I wet the washcloth and put a lot of soap on it. Then I got him all sudsy, especially his hair. I scraped off all the suds and put them in a tin can I had brought. Victor had fun with the suds. Then I filled another can with water and poured it over his head to rinse off the soap. The water was so cold it made him gasp. But he didn't mind because he was having so much fun with his suds. Sometimes he didn't even want to leave.

When the water was shut off, Victor had to have his bath standing in a big tub with just a little water in the bottom. He didn't think that kind of bath was much fun.

In January we heard the sound of planes and gunfire. The skyline at night was lit up with fires. We wondered how much longer it would be before we were rescued.

9

Free at Last!

Every day we saw planes and heard gunfire. But the days went by, and still we were waiting. Everyone was so hungry!

"Unless God does a miracle, many of us may not be here when the soldiers arrive," someone said. "We trust God to work a miracle."

Early on a January morning, a week after New Year's, I woke up in my bunk to hear a noise out in the hall. I sat up in bed and leaned over to look into our living room. Someone was at the hallway door.

"What is it?" asked Mother, on her way to the door.

It was the Clingens from across the hall. "The guards are gone!" they said excitedly. "They heard that our army is very near, so they just ran away."

We could hardly believe our ears. "Were the guards really gone?" we wondered.

The news was so exciting, I could hardly breathe. I jumped out of bed and ran to the door. We hugged each other in our excitement.

The first thing everyone thought of was FOOD! Where was the food? We were sure there were rice and beans close by. The men of the camp went and got them.

News of a wonderful breakfast came from the camp kitchen that morning. We could hardly wait!

But there was something else everyone was thinking about. FREEDOM! We had seen the enemy flag for a long time. How we longed to see the flag of our own country!

Someone brought an American flag from its hiding place. Someone else brought out the Union Jack, the flag of England and Canada. How exciting to see the flags go up on the flagpoles! We sang the national anthems of our countries. As we were singing the British national anthem, I looked over at Mr. Loptson. He was from Canada. His head was lifted, and tears were streaming down his cheeks.

What a breakfast we had! Mush with sugar, coconut mash, and homemade stew! Everyone felt satisfied for the first time in weeks.

In the afternoon someone brought out a radio. Where had they hidden a radio so the guards couldn't find it? They had taken it apart and hidden the pieces in many different places. Now they put the pieces together and tuned it in. For the first time in three years, we heard directly from the United States, our home country.

During the day, many people went to the guards' barracks and brought back food and clothing. Daddy came back with a big sack of coffee beans in his hand. How proud he was of them. He roasted a little every day and then ground the beans.

One day when I was helping in the cookshack, I found some coffee grounds. They had been used at least two times, so I threw them away. Daddy saw they were gone and asked about them. "They could have been used several more times," he said.

The leaders of the camp talked about what we

should do. Some people wanted to leave camp and stay with Filipino friends or go to our army. But the leaders finally decided no one would leave. "Our army is not here yet," they said. "The prison guards might come back. If some of us were gone, they might become angry and punish us. We will stay and wait to see what will happen."

The leaders found many bags of rice. They thought it was a good idea to give each person several pounds. Then if the guards would come back, we would have the extra food.

In a few days, big sacks of rice lay in the hallway of every barracks. Every man, woman, and child received 5 kilos. The 35 kilos our family received almost filled one of the big sacks.

Daddy and Mother talked about all that rice. "We had better hide it around our cubicles," they said. "Then if the guards come back, maybe they won't find it."

Daddy put the rice in many different containers. Then he hid them under the floor in our rooms.

We thanked God for the miracle He had done for us. Several of our missionary families met together across the hall in Clingens' cubicle for prayer and praise. Mr. Loptson read some wonderful verses from Psalms 33, 100, 124, and 126.

After a few days, some more bags of rice were lying in the hallways of each barracks. And soon we would be given even more rice to keep in our rooms.

We had six wonderful days of freedom. Then the guards came back at 2:30 in the morning!

"Bring back the shovels and shoes and other things you took from our barracks," they said. So the men returned whatever they could take back.

The guards found the sacks of rice in the hall-ways. "Bring that rice back," they said. Sadly the men did as they were told. But no one said anything about the rice hidden in our cubicles. The guards never asked about it either. God was taking care of us.

The rest of January went by. Then February. There was still gunfire, and planes flew overhead. There were more fires at night. And food was scarce again. We thanked God for the hidden rice. But we didn't want to eat it too soon. We didn't know when "our boys" would come to rescue us.

For a long time we hadn't had roll call. Now we had to come out in front of our barracks each morning to be counted. Some days we had roll call two or three times. That was hard for those who were weak and sick.

One day the guards told us there was no more food. All they had for us was palay (puh-LIE)—rice with the husk still on.

"But how can we get the husks off?" our leaders asked the guards. "It's palay or nothing," the guards answered.

The leaders decided to give each person a pow-dered milk can full of palay. That was the amount for two days. Each family would have to decide how to get the husks off!

This was a state of emergency. Everyone gathered in their cubicles to work at husking the rice. The chil-dren had been attending some classes. Now school was closed. Preparing food was more important than anything else.

The Filipinos had a way of husking rice. They beat the husks off with big, rounded poles. But we didn't have anything like that. We had to use any ideas we had.

71

And everyone had an idea. "I think the best way is to rub the rice between two boards," one person said.

"That's too slow," said someone else. "I think pounding it with a big stone is better." And so it went.

In our dining area, all the Hess children sat around the table. Daddy pounded and rubbed to get the husks off. Then we children carefully put all the husked grain into containers. We gave the unhusked grains back to Daddy to work on again. It was slow work. And we were all weak from hunger.

Daddy and Mother still were not feeling well. After one day's work, we still hadn't finished husking tomorrow's ration.

The next day after roll call, we had rice for breakfast—some from our hidden store. How thankful we were to have some left. Many people had eaten all they had. For lunch we had the freshly husked rice with a little gravy.

It was a strange day. All day long our planes dropped bombs on the other side of a nearby hill.

What did it mean? "I think it has something to do with us," Daddy said. We watched and wondered.

"Let's meet together this afternoon to pray," the missionaries said to each other. They came to our cubicle. What a wonderful meeting it was. The Lord was so near. We knew He was watching over us.

The next morning people were up getting ready for roll call and breakfast.

"I think I'll put the rice on so it can be cooking while we are at roll call," Daddy said. "I guess the coffee can wait until after roll call."

He put some of the precious rice from under the floor on to cook. We had not finished husking the rest of the palay the day before.

"Hurry and get ready for roll call," Mother said to me. "Some people have already gone out." I got my comb and started to go to the washhouse. Suddenly someone pointed up to the sky above our roof. We all looked up.

We saw the black shapes of airplanes against the sunrise. Then as we watched, small, black specks began falling from the planes.

"What are they, Daddy?" we asked. Before he could answer, we saw for ourselves. They were parachutes opening up and gently falling out of sight behind the trees.

Plane after plane flew across the morning sunrise. Little, black parachutes fell from each one. We stared, without moving, until all the planes were gone.

We wondered what it all meant. But it was almost seven o'clock. I hurried to the washhouse to comb my hair. Suddenly there was gunfire—right in our camp!

I ran back to our cubicle. The men had dug a long ditch along the side of our barracks. Quickly, we jumped into the ditch. All up and down our side of the barracks we could see people getting into the ditch.

Lois looked along the ditch and saw her little friend. She raised her head to wave at her. "Put your head down," Mother said.

The Clingens across the hall were hiding under their beds. Suddenly I heard Mr. Clingen call, "Welcome, soldier boy!"

Could it be? Yes, our soldiers were walking through the barracks. We all rushed up to them. We didn't understand what was happening.

Then someone explained. These were paratroopers! They had dropped near our camp and, with Filipino soldiers, surrounded the prison guards, and

took over our camp. OUR BOYS had come! And not a moment too soon!!

Later we discovered that the camp commander had orders to kill all the prisoners at roll call that morning. Our soldiers found out about the plan and had sent the paratroopers just in time to rescue us.

But there wasn't time for celebration now. "Hurry and pack the few things you need," our soldiers said. "The enemy is not far away. We want to get you out before they have a chance to come back.

"Gather your things and start walking toward the lake. We will have amphibian tanks to take you across the lake to our army base."

It was almost too much for us. We were terribly excited, but everyone was weak, and many were sick. We packed some things but could hardly carry them. Almost before we had left our barracks, the soldiers set fire to them. I followed Daddy down the dirt road, sobbing and crying. Daddy was so weak. His legs could hardly hold him up. How could he carry that heavy load on his back?

As we walked, I looked around. People had thrown things away all along the road. They thought they wouldn't need them anymore.

I saw a large cone of string. How I wished to have it. Then I remembered we didn't need those things now. We were free! We could get plenty of things like that when we got back home.

Then I saw a can of Spam and a can of corned beef lying beside a tree. Someone had saved those cans from their Red Cross food boxes. I couldn't bear to leave the food sitting there. I hurried over and picked the cans up.

"Look, Mother," I said. "I found two cans of meat."

"Hang on to them," she answered. "We can have them for our lunch."

Some people had hurriedly started walking toward the lake. The first amphibian tanks came and picked them up. By the time we got there, there were no more tanks. We would have to wait until the others came back.

"Don't wait here," the soldiers said. They were very anxious. "The enemy might come back any minute. Just leave your baggage here. We will try to bring it later. Start walking to the lake and wait there."

So we began to walk. A soldier walked with us and carried Victor. Suddenly a shot rang out. The soldier quickly handed Victor back to Daddy and ran off, his hand on his gun. We jumped into the ditch until things got quiet again.

Soon a truck came by and picked us up. We arrived at the lakeshore and waited for the amphibian tanks.

In the meantime, some Filipinos came up selling food. Mother bought some eggs. Then she opened the cans of meat and mixed in the raw egg. She quickly fed us the mixture. We might have to go right away.

After a while, we could see the amphibian tanks coming back across the lake. They came up on land and let down a big ramp in the back. We all walked into the tank. There was room only to stand. Mother was carrying a bag that had very special things in it—our Bible, medicines, Daddy's diary. Everything else had been left behind. Mother said she wasn't going to let that bag out of her hand.

After a short trip across the lake, big trucks took us to our army base at a prison building called New Bilibid. There we got into an American chow line for supper.

We had vegetable soup. But how different it was from the soup we had been eating at camp. "Look, Mother," I said, "there are peas and carrots in this soup." I hadn't seen peas and carrots in years.

"That's right," Mother answered. "Now eat your soup."

"But, Mother, I can't believe it's real peas and carrots!"

"I know," Mother answered patiently. "It's wonderful. Now eat your soup."

The next day I found out that after we children went to bed, the adults went back through the chow line three or four times! The boys who were serving the food just couldn't turn them down. How wonderful to have enough food again!

We stayed at New Bilibid for about three weeks. Every day we were able to eat a little more, as our stomachs got used to more food. We were given new clothes, and some coats and sweaters for winter. It would be cold on the ship and back home in the States when we returned.

I helped Mother with sewing. I made a dress for myself and some clothes for the others. We had to make some of the new clothes fit.

How much fun we had with our soldiers. We begged them all the time for chewing gum and candy bars. The boys had fun riding around on the trucks and jeeps. And we had popcorn in the evenings! It all seemed too good to be true.

At last the day came when we were to sail home to the States. We looked forward to seeing our grandparents and other relatives again.

When we got back home, many friends said to us, "We knew you would come home. Your grandmother prayed for you every day. She told us, 'God will be with my children in the Philippines. He will bring them home safely.'"

Then we knew, more than ever, that it was God's Word and prayer that had saved us. The Lord had protected us and kept us alive. Believing God and His Word made all the difference.

Epilogue

Would you like to know what happened to the Hess children when they grew up?

Philip, youngest of the six children, was born to Robert and Viola Hess after the war. He grew up in the Philippines and attended Faith Academy in Manila. He lives in Minnesota and is active in his mission-minded local church. He is married to Ruth Ann and they have two children.

Victor became a missionary pilot in the jungles of Panama and Colombia, South America, and more recently in Cameroon, Africa. He flies airplanes to help missionaries who translate the Bible in other languages. Vic is married to Val, and they have three children.

Lois became a teacher of second grade boys and girls. For several years she taught missionary children in Quito, Ecuador. She married Bernie Lupole and lives in New York State. They have a business selling Christian books and operate a camp bookstore during the summer.

Bruce became a missionary in Colombia and Ecuador, South America. He helped start new churches and trained young people to become pastors. Bruce is married to Donna, and they have three children. Bruce and Donna now live in Pennsylvania, where they are regional directors of OMS International, a missionary organization. They challenge God's people, young and old, to consider doing short- or long-term missionary service.

Hudson worked in Japan and then became a missionary in Haiti and France with OMS International. He helped prepare radio programs for radio station 4-VEH and trained pastors. Hudson is married to Lucy, and they have six children. They do missionary work in Haiti.

Arlene wrote Sunday School lessons for several years for children in the United States. Arlene is married to Ken Elkins and lives in Kansas City, Kansas. She now works at the Nazarene headquarters.

Hess children, (left to right)
Philip, Hudson, Arlene, Victor, and Bruce with Lois in front

Prisoners of War
The capture and rescue adventure
of a missionary family
A true story from World War II
by R. Bruce Hess

War

Growing up on the other side of the world has its disadvantages, especially when the world goes to war. It crashed upon us like an ocean wave over the rock-covered shore. Dad and Mom went to the Philippine Islands in 1932 as missionaries. But why did I have to come into this world of turmoil, starvation, deprivation and death? Where could I find escape and freedom? Hope was so distant.

Capture

My earliest recollections are of our simple home in the tropics of the Philippines and then our escape with a small missionary group, with the help of trusted Filipinos, to our hideout in the Mindanao jungles. This was during World War II, which began with the bombing of Pearl Harbor on December 7, 1941. I had my 6th birthday in the jungle and began my first days of primary school in what today we would call "home schooling."

My first conscious encounter with death occurred when my small foot slipped into a crevice where a poisonous snake was coiled to strike. Like a whisper from heaven these words came to me, "I have spared your life. I want you to serve me." I pulled my foot back and ran for safety. Later, I began to realize that life is not by chance, but it is under the order and control of an all-powerful God who directs all of history and knows us completely. King David wrote in Psalm 139:16, "...your eyes saw my unformed body.. All the days ordained for me were written in your book before one of them came to be." (NIV) Little did I know then what was ahead and how much more I would have to learn about God and His watchful eye.

After 13 months of hiding in the jungle, the enemy soldiers came for us, surrounded our jungle hideout early one morning and ordered us to pack what we could and begin marching. For the next 2 1/2 years our family, and many others, were held in prison camps in the cities of Zamboanga, Davao, Manila and Los Banos.

Prisoner

Dad and Mom had come to the Philippines to tell the people how Christ could change their lives, taking them from their sins to freedom, life and hope in Jesus. Jesus says, "The thief does not come except to steal, and to kill, and to destroy. I have come that they may have life, and that they may have it more abundantly." (John 10:10) Their lives and work were interrupted while they and we five children were prisoners of war.

Even as a small boy, I began to see the results of sin in the world and in the hearts of men and women. Hatred, bloodshed, starvation, suffering and death were all around. Inside the prison, even if I only went to the fence line, I could get shot. Did I have a future? Would I ever grow up? Was this what life had to offer me?

I learned from the Bible that being a prisoner was only one kind of slavery. Evil in the heart of man would lead not only to physical death, but eternal death, too, as it says in Romans 3:23 and Romans 6:23,

"...for all have sinned and fall short of the glory of God..." and "For the wages of sin is death, but the gift of God is eternal life in Christ Jesus our Lord." These words included me, even though I had been taught what was right and wrong, from the cradle, by my parents Mother had assured me that just because my parents were missionaries; this would not secure a place in heaven for me. It was up to me! My choice! I couldn't get to heaven on my mother's faith. I was in spiritual bondage.

One day my older brother and I went to dig "cassava" roots (similar to potatoes) for food. Since the guard nearest us had given permission, we set to work with our hands and a large knife called a "bolo." Without warning an enemy soldier outside the camp fence arrived, spotted us digging and began yelling at us and pointing his rifle. I wanted to start running but Hudson said, "Give me the bolo to cut off this root." We were hungry, and I was scared—scared of dying. I knew that just a slight move of that soldier's trigger finger, and it would all be over for me. A voice, as though from heaven, said to me, "I have saved your life. I want you to work for me."

I knew the Bible story of little Samuel, who, when he heard the voice of God, responded, "Speak, for your servant is listening." (I Samuel 3:10, NIV) So I realized I must pray to God, turn from doing things my own way, and follow Him to have everlasting life. Jesus came, was born in a stable, lived a sinless life and died a sacrificial death on the cross to give us all eternal life. Jesus, who was raised from the dead, is powerful enough to provide us eternal life. Jesus said, "I am the way, the truth, and the life. No one comes to the Father except through Me." (John 14:6)

Starvation

Everyone in the camp thought of only two things: **food** and **freedom**. The final weeks we were given only unshelled rice called "palay" (pronounced puh-LIE). No pestle and mortar or winnowing basket was available to shell the rice. Each family used boards or stones doing the tedious work by hand. Some of the older men cooked the "palay" without shelling it, but when they tried to eat it, the hulls tore into their digestive tracks so terribly that they became very ill.

An ex-prisoner explained, "We prayed and we waited. This was the worst we had experienced so far, the waiting and the starvation. Our bodies were so malnourished from only two portions of watery rice gruel a day that there was real doubt that we could hold on until we were liberated." All I remember at age eight and a half is the gnawing, relentless hunger every minute night and day.

Rescue

On February 23, 1945, we prisoners hesitated to line up for early morning roll call because it had been rumored that everyone was to be shot at that time. Suddenly the bullets began to fly. Our family ran to the security ditches, got in and crouched down while bullets flew overhead. One ex-prisoner reported, "Oh, what a wonderful sight it was when the American soldiers came in. They told us, 'Grab your things—we're taking you out.' And they did. We took what we could with us, and they put us on amphibious tanks and headed us out. There was still shooting and fighting all around."

My sister Arlene explained it this way. "Could it be? Yes, our soldiers were walking through the barracks. We all rushed up to them. We didn't understand what was happening."

Then someone explained that these soldiers were paratroopers. They dropped from airplanes near our camp and, with Filipino soldiers, surrounded the prison guards and took over our camp. Our men had come! And not a moment too soon!!

Yes, we were free, but not out of danger. Our family didn't make it on the first trip of the amphibious tanks. We were told to start walking to the bay (2 miles away) where the tanks would pick us up on their return trip. Dad and Mom were so weak. Every step was like trudging in mud. Some soldiers walked with us urging us along. In a flash, a shot rang out. The soldier who was carrying my baby brother Victor, (2 1/2 years old) swung around, set him down, grabbing his rifle in hand, advanced to the opposite side of the road while shouting, "Sniper! Dive for the ditch."

Like a dart the thought pierced my troubled mind, "You thought you were getting out! The sniper will get you." As though in response, a voice from heaven again responded, "I saved your life. I want you to work for me."

Some say that the most dramatic part of the war experience is the CAPTURE. If that is true, which I doubt, certainly the most incredible and awesome aspect is the RESCUE. One minute I was a prisoner, then the next, I was escaping to freedom. My mind and heart were on overload with every emotion possible — hope, disbelief, uncertainty (is it for real?), expectancy, excitement, etc.

Spiritual Bondage and Freedom

I feel the same way about my spiritual life. Even as a small boy, I was captive to my own worst fears— of suffering, hopelessness and death. I wondered if I would live to grow up and if I died, would I go to heaven. When I turned my life over to Jesus Christ the outcome was equally dramatic. Placing my trust completely in Jesus meant I was free from sin, guilt and spiritual death. For God says in 2 Corinthians 5:17, "When someone becomes a Christian he becomes a brand new person inside. He is not the same anymore. A new life has begun!" (LIV)

I experienced that new life when I was 13. A few weeks before leaving the Philippines for high school and college in the States, my mother had prayer with me. She asked, "Have you made a commitment once and for all to follow Jesus?" I wasn't sure, although I knew I had raised my hand and gone forward for prayer in church meetings. "Do you want to make a decision now?" she inquired. I said yes, and we prayed.

From that time on I have continued to follow the Lord. He has never left me in my weak times or strong times. I want to serve Him always. He gave me a scripture in Deuteronomy 33:27, "The eternal God is your refuge, and underneath are the everlasting arms; He will thrust out the enemy from before you,..."

What Have I Learned?

I knew after an experience like this, my life would never be the same again. I wholeheartedly agree with ex-prisoner Sascha Jean who in 1995 wrote, "The experience during the war never leaves my mind for very long. I don't dwell on it to be sure, however, there are daily occurrences that remind me of incidents during our imprisonment."

I learned an adult outlook as a child. I learned to appreciate everything, take nothing for granted or waste anything. Something changes inside when you have no medicine, no food, no clothing, nothing. People become significant.

In my spiritual life I learned the truth of Romans 5:8, that God loved me first, even when I didn't know Him. When I prayed to Him, He was there waiting to receive me as His son. "...God has given us eternal life, and this life is in His Son. He who has the Son has life, he who does not have the Son of God does not have life." (1 John 5:11-12)

He filled my life with new purpose and my heart with His love for others. I'll never be the same again because God's Spirit entered my life to abide with me forever. (Romans 8:11-14) Jesus is always with me. (Matthew 28:20)

What About You?

Have you ever heard that voice from heaven in your heart or mind inviting you to seek after Him? Life is short at best, and death is certain. Jesus Christ has new life and a beautiful and fruitful plan for your life. You don't enter heaven by chance. You enter by specific request. "Ask and it will be given to you..." (Matthew 7:7-8)

Do you believe in Him? Will you take the step from sin and captivity by Satan to God and spiritual freedom? The invitation is specific and clear. "Come to Me, all you who labor and are heavy laden, and I will give you rest." (Matthew 11:28) Jesus is ready to rescue you. You must follow Him out of the camp of the enemy. Begin by making the following words your prayer: "God in Heaven, I come to tell You that I have sinned against You and am a sinner by nature. You have promised to change my life forever if I will humble myself and believe in You and Your Son, Jesus Christ, as my Savior. Please forgive me and save me now by Your grace. This I ask in Jesus' name. Amen."

I John 1:9 says, "If we confess our sins He is faithful and just to forgive us our sins, and cleanse us from all unrighteousness." Your sincere honest confession will bring God's trustworthy response.

If you've taken this first step, it is exciting to know that this is just a beginning. God has entered your life and wants to show you how to grow spiritually. I hope you will read the Bible and find a local church where you will learn how to live with Christ as your Lord.

Please write and tell me what God has done for you. I will rejoice with you on your RESCUE FROM SATAN'S CAPTIVITY, and I will pray for you.

(All Bible quotations are from the New King James Version unless specified.)

R. Bruce Hess, Northeast Regional Director
OMS International, Inc.,1705 E. Greenleaf St.
Allentown, PA 18109

The Miracle of a Song
Another Capture and Rescue Adventure
by Hudson Hess

As snowflakes soon melt on a warm cheek, the Christmas season usually flits quickly across our lives, leaving warm memories and some sadness because it is so soon gone. On rare occasions a special Christmas towers above the others with meaning and beauty, which lingers long after it has gone. Such was the Christmas of 1943 for me.

Our family had been captured in the Philippines by Japanese forces at the outbreak of World War II. After 13 months in hiding we were betrayed by nationals and subsequently taken into captivity. For a few months we were held in our hometown of Zamboanga. Then, accompanied by a number of other missionary families, we were taken to Davao City on the southern coast of Mindanao Island.

Our place of prison was an old dance hall a few miles outside the city. At first glance the well-kept grounds and large buildings gave the impression of a country club. But closer view evidenced its sore need of repair. Over the main entrance a faded sign read: "Happy Life Blues."

Inside, a large, open hall had been stripped of all furnishings. At the far end a pair of staircases led to a balcony. Chalk lines crisscrossed the main floor to form rectangles, each inscribed with the name of the family assigned to it. We were told to find our spot and deposit our belongings. All day long truckloads of people arrived, until some 250 huddled among their few possessions at their appointed spot. As citizens of countries warring with Japan, we were brought in from all over southern Philippines. Some of the older men were veterans of the Spanish-American War.

The first night in the dance hall was awful. Babies cried in the stifling heat while their mothers tried to comfort them. Then some old man would shout, "Choke it," and everyone would wake up. Angry words flew back and forth, and people crawled over each other in the darkness to find their way to the restrooms.

In following days the men went out to the swamps, under armed guard, to get materials for making partitions and building furniture. Gradually my father's ingenuity and hard work paid off. Our rectangle became an enclosed room, complete with a double-deck double bed for my two sisters and my brother, Bruce and me, a crib for baby Victor, a wide bed for Mother and Dad and some chairs.

Although we now had a measure of comfort and privacy, the nightly bedlam continued. Every conversation had to be whispered for fear of disturbing neighbors, and we could still hear everything that went on in the cubicles around us. Finally Dad had enough. He announced that he had received permission from authorities to build a small house (hut) out on the grounds. He also asked another missionary family, the Bresslers, to join us.

Each day the guards followed the men as they went to gather timbers, while we children wove palm fronds for the walls and roof. One day the men were tearing down an old house. Dad was working in the attic while others ripped out walls below. Suddenly amid shouts, the house collapsed. Those below scrambled to safety but Dad had to ride the rubble as it fell. Two rafters, coming together above his head, snatched his helmet off and smashed it flat. But Dad was unharmed. That evening when he threw his helmet on the bed a horrible feeling swept over me; I realized how close we came to losing him that day.

Sometime in November we moved into our new house. Although it was nothing more than the most primitive of huts it seemed like a palace. What a relief to get out of the dance hall! We had so much to be thankful for. Our family was all together and we were well. We could sleep without interruption now, for nights were cool, and we were free from the commotion in the hall. Naturally our thoughts turned toward Christmas and the celebration of our Savior's birth. We began to make plans.

First of all we thought of presents. Since we couldn't go shopping, we decided to make things for each other. Dad worked on wooden clogs for the ladies, a high chair for Victor, and other secret projects. I made a checker set for my big sister, Arlene, and designed a set of paper dolls for Lois. All the secrecy, hard work and glorious anticipation were great fun.

Mother made special arrangements with the guards to get ingredients for cookies, and the camp negotiated the purchase of a steer to be carved into steaks for Christmas dinner. (Normally we received only the blood, guts and refuse from the slaughterhouse for our meals.) Some of the adults also worked with the children on a special program to be presented on the front steps of "The Blues" during Christmas week.

The day before the big event, last minute preparations were in full swing and excitement ran so high it saturated our very bones. This would be the best Christmas we ever had. We just knew it!

Without the slightest warning, however, our happy dreams came crashing down. At 10:00 a.m. on December 24 the loud speakers blared. We were ordered to assemble immediately on the front lawn and to line up by families in alphabetical order. A guard checked the camp list to make sure all were present. Then came the devastating news: "You'll be shipped to Manila today. Pack only what you can carry and report back by 2:00 p.m., ready to board trucks." It just couldn't be true! How could this happen?

We were numb with disappointment. Little time was available to mourn our losses, however. It took all the speed we could muster to pack our few valuables and be back in line on time.

I was thrust up front with the driver. This looked like fun. But the truck was old and required a full turn-and-a-half of the wheel in order to register the slightest alteration in the vehicle's course. Our convoy followed a hilly stretch of road full of hairpin curves, our truck, all the while, wandering from one side to the other as though our driver were drunk. I breathed a sigh of relief when we finally arrived at the shore, where some freighters were docked.

The ship to which we were directed sat high in the water and was rusting badly. We filed up the gangplank to a large, flat deck. I wondered for a moment where our cabins would be. Then it struck me. We were being moved quickly into the hold. As I started down the ladder into that dark interior, fear encased me.

A series of shelves had been constructed on both sides of the hold from the bottom to the top. Each shelf was fastened to a bulkhead at the back and extended almost to the center of the ship, leaving a gap of about five feet between it and its companion shelf on the opposite side. This gap provided ventilation to the hold and served as the means of access by way of ladders fastened to the sides of the shelves. The shelves were only about three feet apart and were covered with straw matting. A large number of life preservers were strewn about, but they could serve only as pillows. Certainly they'd never be used as flotation devices since none of us could have escaped if the ship went down.

The poor souls whose names began with *A* went to the very bottom of the ship. Since ours began with *H* we fared some better. Our level shelf was about halfway up the port side. I slithered all the way back and lay still on a life preserver. I was sure our lives were about to come to an end. The heat was unbearable. Fortunately, night was coming on when they closed the doors and got underway.

I'll not forget that night as long as I live. It was Christmas Eve. We were sealed like bodies in a tomb with darkness so thick we could feel it. Absolutely no sound could be heard. Not even a baby whimpered. A terrible feeling gripped us all. Only a week before, U.S. submarines had sunk two ships at this very place. Was one out there waiting for us?

I have no idea how long the oppressive silence lasted. But suddenly, from the very bowels of the ship, a male voice drifted up to us: "Silent Night, Holy Night, all is calm, all is bright…." Another voice joined in and then another. Louder and louder they sang until the whole interior of that ship reverberated with hundreds of voices singing the beloved Christmas carol.

For a terrified boy in his cubbyhole that night, a miracle took place. Immediately the whole, dank interior of the black hold was transformed into a place of beauty. It seemed that I was seated in a large amphitheater domed by a sky of twinkling stars. With fluttering wings an angel appeared and began to sing. Presently he was joined by another and yet another, until a vast choir of angels filled the place with song. As their voices grew ever louder, I was transported out of that dismal place into the very presence of God. A sense of peace and well-being washed over me, and I knew with full assurance that we would be all right.

The carol singing went on for a long, long time. Then, all at once, the hatch above us was thrown open and a Japanese sailor, evidently drunk, called down to us. He was scared, too, poor fellow. But, oh, how refreshing was the cool air from above, as it descended upon us like a shower. We sang another number for the sailor, and he clapped. Then he sang a Japanese song for us, and we applauded. This continued for some time. Realizing that our supply of fresh air depended upon the presence of our unknown entertainer, we urged him on by cheering heartily after each song. I've often wondered if that dear man ever came to know the loving Savior we sang about that night.

Aside from my mother giving Victor a bath in tea the next day (since fresh water was not available), I don't remember much about that trip. Yes, we had a gift exchange of sorts on Christmas day and sampled Mother's cookies. But the memories of that experience and the lessons learned will stay with me forever. There *is* power in Christian singing, which can make miracles happen in our darkened world. And the mystique of Christmas comes not from the things we give and get, but from the joy of being alive together and celebrating in God's and each other's presence.

MISSION TO THE MAX

For more information about the Philippines or Christian missionary work around the world, contact the Children's Ministry Department of OMS International. OMS offers an interesting children's publication called **Missions to the MAX** which takes children to a different OMS country each quarter. Children's mission projects called **Kids Can Do** (and big people, too!) are also available. Contact:
Children's Ministry, OMS International
Box A, Greenwood, IN 46142
max@omsinternational.org
Phone: 317-881-6751

OTHER "CAPTURED" MATERIAL

Two companion items to this book are also available: "Captured: A Read-Along Coloring Book" and "Captured, A True Christmas Story." The latter, a Christmas play, is written for school and church mission events. The "Hess Family Tale" will stir everyone's heart to thankfulness for Christ's birth and then for His continuing provisions for all of us. For copies of *Captured*, the coloring book or the Christmas play, contact Bruce Hess at 610-434-7359, or bhess@omsinternational.org or contact OMS.

ABOUT OMS

OMS International is an interdenominational faith mission emphasizing culturally sensitive evangelism, training national leadership for ministry and church planting in Africa, Asia, the Caribbean, Europe and Latin America.

Each of more than 450 OMS missionaries trusts God to provide his support through the prayers and gifts of His people.

OMS works in partnership with over 7,941 national workers and 5,572 organized churches whose membership exceeds one million. In 32 seminaries and Bible training schools, 6,841 students are preparing for ministry. Through going everywhere to tell people about Jesus, 343 teams lead thousands to Christ and assist in establishing over four new churches each week.

For information regarding scholarships for seminary students, adopting a missionary or country, visiting ministry sites, sending youth teams, or personal short-term and long-term ministry opportunities, please write OMS International, Box A, Greenwood, Indiana 46142-6599 or info@omsinternational.org or call 317-881-6751. You may also visit our website at www.omsinternational.org

Dedicated to my parents,
Robert R. and Viola R. Hess,
whose faith and trust in God
and His Word
have given me confidence and hope
throughout my life.